Topsy + Tim

Red Boots, Yellow Boots

Jean and Gareth Adamson

When Topsy and Tim looked out of the window for the first time on Monday morning the rain was *pouring* down.

The moral rights of the author and illustrator have been asserted

A catalogue record for this book is available
from the British Library

Published by Ladybird Books Ltd
A subsidiary of the Penguin Group
A Pearson Company

© Jean and Gareth Adamson MCMXCVII

LADYBIRD and the device of a Ladybird are trademarks of
Ladybird Books Ltd Loughborough Leicestershire UK

Mr Fen, who lived next door, was
holding a big, stripey umbrella.

"Nice weather – for ducks!" he called.

Two pairs of boots were standing in the hall—yellow boots for Topsy and red boots for Tim.

"I'm not wearing *my* boots," said Tim.

Mummy pulled and Topsy pushed –
and Topsy had her boots on, ready
to go to playgroup.

"Now you, Tim," said Mummy.

Tim was very naughty and stamped and shouted, *"I don't want my boots."*

"All right," said Mummy. "You can wear your ordinary shoes. It's time you learned a lesson."

So when Tim and Topsy set off for playgroup, Topsy was wearing her big yellow boots but Tim was wearing his ordinary shoes.

Tim could run faster in his ordinary
shoes, so he danced in circles round
Topsy shouting, "Funny boots!
Funny boots!"

Tim walked backwards in front of
Topsy and put out his tongue.

And then he stepped right into a
deep, deep, puddle.

"Yow!" he howled. "My feet are all cold and wet."

Topsy walked right through the big puddle and didn't get cold or wet at all.

"Come inside quickly, children,"
called Miss Maypole, "and change
into your dry shoes."

"Whyever aren't you wearing your
big red boots, Tim?" asked
Miss Maypole.

"He wouldn't put them on," laughed
Topsy.

"What a silly little boy!" said
Miss Maypole. "I shall have to hang
your wet socks up to dry."

Tim had to sit on a table with his
bare feet dangling.

When Mummy came to fetch them home she had Tim's big red boots in her zip-up bag.

He put them on quickly.

Topsy and Tim plodged through all
the big puddles on the way home.

"Good old red boots!" said Tim.

Talk about the story.

Tim's boots are red.
Topsy's boots are yellow.

Can you match the pairs here?

Topsy and Tim planted some seeds.

Talk about what happened after that.

Topsy and Tim are looking for the
missing words in these rhymes
about the rain.

Can you say the words?

Rain, , go away
Come again another day.

Incy Wincy
Climbed up the spout.
Down came a rain storm,
And washed the out.
When the came out again,
And dried up all the
Incy Wincy Spider climbed the spout again.

Help Topsy and Tim to work out
the puzzles.

Which is wet?
Which is dry?

Which is up?
Which is down?

Which is on?
Which is off?

Which is high?
Which is low?